Witch-in-Training

Training

Charming or What?

Maeve Friel

Illustrated by Nathan Reed

ROARING GOOD READS

Collins

An imprint of HarperCollinsPublishers

First published by Collins in 2003
Collins is an imprint of HarperCollins*Publishers* Ltd
77-85 Fulham Palace Road, Hammersmith, London W6 8JB

The HarperCollins website address is www.**fire**and**water**.com

1 3 5 7 9 8 6 4 2

Text copyright © Maeve Friel 2003

Illustrations by Nathan Reed 2003

ISBN 0 00 713343 X

The author asserts the moral right to be
identified as the author of the work.

Printed and bound in England by
Clays Ltd, St Ives plc

Witch Training

Training

Charming or What?

ROARING GOOD READS

Collins

An imprint of HarperCollinsPublishers

Also by Maeve Friel.
Witch-in-Training: Flying Lessons
Witch-in-Training: Spelling Trouble

Coming soon:
Witch-in-Training: Brewing Up

Other Roaring Good Reads from Collins

Mister Skip *by Michael Morpurgo*
Daisy May *by Jean Ure*
The Witch's Tears *by Jenny Nimmo*
Spider McDrew *by Alan Durant*
Dazzling Danny *by Jean Ure*

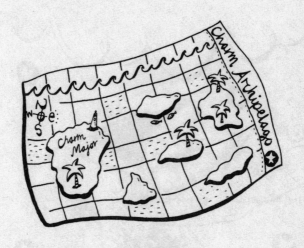

Chapter One

A cold raindrop slid down Jessica's nose.

"Bother," she grumbled. "I hate flying in the rain."

Jessica was on her way to Miss Strega's shop on the High Street where she was

about to begin her third course of lessons as a witch-in-training. She had already learnt to fly a broomstick (the right way up) and had even vaulted over the moon. She was pretty good at Spelling (with and without a wand) and knew how to make a basic brew. She had a terrific flying helmet and a Super-Duper De-Luxe Guaranteed-Invisibility -When-You-Need-It cape. Unfortunately, both the cape and the helmet were letting in water.

"Bother and double bother," she repeated as she wiped her nose. "I should have taken the bus."

Berkeley, Jessica's night-in-gale mascot, poked her head out of Jessica's pocket. "Hu-eet, hu-eet," she chirruped sweetly and cocked an eye at the broom's *Fast-Forward* twig.

"We *are* Fast Forwarding, silly," Jessica sniffed. "And stop singing. It's not singing weather."

Berkeley quickly snuggled back into her warm pocket fluff and they flew on without another tweet. Jessica buried her chin in her cape, pulled her flying helmet down over her eyes and grimly steered her broom forward until she was directly above Miss Strega's hardware shop. She dropped down, dismounted and immediately stepped into a deep puddle. As she lifted the latch of the shop door, a huge drop of water fell off the

creaking shop sign and trickled down the back of her neck. She stomped inside.

Old Miss Strega was sitting as usual on her high stool behind the counter. She had her long chin cupped comfortably in one hand and held a book in the other. Felicity, Miss Strega's ginger cat, was sitting in her usual place on top of a pile of Spell Books.

As Jessica dripped across the shop floor, Miss Strega looked up and peered at her over her glasses. "You're making puddles, Jessica."

Jessica pulled out her wand. She frowned with concentration as she tried to think of a suitable Wash 'n' Wipe Spell.

"NO Spelling," Miss Strega warned. "I don't want you flooding my shop by mistake and holding up our flight. There's a mop under the stairs."

Jessica scowled as she fetched the mop. "What flight?"

Miss Strega tapped the cover of the *Witches World Wide Rule Book*. "It says here that witches-in-training should spend some time abroad so I've booked—"

"A holiday?" Jessica stopped mopping and spun around. "What a brilliant idea."

"Well, not exactly a holiday." Miss Strega cleared her throat. "At least, not for you. I've put your name down for a summer school."

Jessica raised a damp eyebrow. "A summer school? To learn what?"

"Why, Charming of course," declared Miss Strega, hopping down from her stool.

"You certainly need some Charm skills and Pelagia's Academy in the Charm Archipelago is the very best. Felicity and I will come too. And Berkeley."

"Felicity and Berkeley and *you* are going to school too?"

"Moonrays and marrowbones!" Miss Strega cackled. "Of course not. We three already know everything there is to know about Charming. *We* shall be on holiday."

At the mention of her name, Berkeley fluttered out of Jessica's pocket and enthusiastically trilled thank you in her lovely silvery voice.

Felicity winked an orange eye at Jessica.

Jessica stuck her tongue out at the cat and turned to Miss Strega who was noisily emptying a drawer full of her own wands on to the counter. "Who is this Pelagia anyway?"

"Pelagia is rather an unusual witch. She used to be a

pirate, but had a change of heart for some reason and decided to be good. She's a lighthouse keeper now and teaches Charming part-time."

"Do I have to do Charming? Isn't Spelling enough?"

Miss Strega stroked her long chin. "Personally, I suggest you try both. You see, Charming is not something everybody can pick up, like flying a broomstick or typing without looking at the keyboard or making a basic brew. Charming is more a way of *being*, it's something you *become*."

Jessica looked confused.

"And then again," Miss Strega continued, "you will need to know about Charms. They can be *incantations* but they can also be *things*. Like a lucky horseshoe or a magic crystal."

Jessica looked more confused than ever. Was Pelagia going to make her *become a horseshoe*, rather like *being a tree* at drama lessons?

Miss Strega stuck a wand behind her ear and gathered the rest into a bundle with a rubber band. "Look, don't worry your bewitching little head about it for the moment, Jess. Pelagia will explain all this much better than I can. So let's shut up the shop and take to the sky."

Felicity and Berkeley sat on the counter and watched with interest as Jessica and Miss Strega prepared for their trip. First of all, Jessica put away the mop and filed the bundle of Miss Strega's own wands in a drawer marked *My Swansdown*. (This was an example of Noquan – Not Quite An Anagram – one of Miss Strega's highly secret codes to hide what she really had for sale if non-witches blundered into the shop.) Then while Miss Strega made up a flask of her favourite brew, Cold Smelly Voles, for the journey, Jessica carefully sprayed her broomstick with goblin deterrent. (She still got the heebie-jeebies when she remembered the night that she had had to eject a goblin that had cheekily clambered on to her broomstick.)

Miss Strega counted all the groats and maravedis in the till and tipped them into her saddle bag. Jessica topped up the bird seed in her pocket. Finally, Miss Strega riffled through a box of cards beside the door.

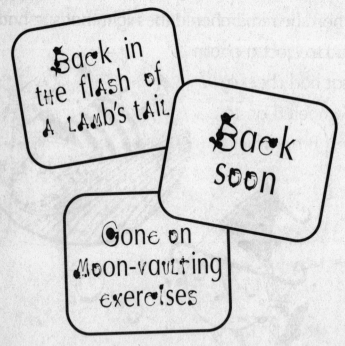

Back in the flash of a lamb's tail

Back soon

Gone on Moon-vaulting exercises

"No good, no good, no good. Ah-ha, this one will be perfect," she said, selecting a card and looping it over a nail on the door. "Now, Felicity, Berkeley, Jessica, take your positions, prepare for take-off. Ig-Fo-Li: Ignition, Forward and Lift."

Jessica pressed her *Ignition* twig and eased her broom forward. As the door closed quietly behind her, she turned around to read the notice.

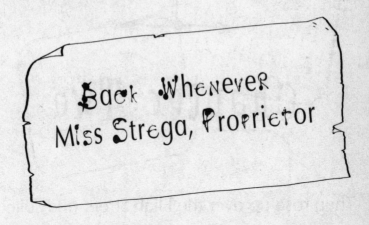

Back Whenever
Miss Strega, Proprietor

Chapter Two

They rose up over the High Street and sailed over the park where, only months earlier, Jessica had made her first flight. The rain, if anything, was worse. Frogs croaked and splashed off into the duck pond, a sopping fox rummaged in a rubbish bin. Owls huddled and shivered in their tree boxes. All the neighbourhood cats had gone home out of the wet.

"Brrr," thought Jessica, "I hope it will be warmer in the Charm archi-thingy."

With the wind behind them, the broomsticks made fast progress and they were soon flying over international waters. Gradually, the rain stopped, the mist cleared and the sun shone brightly. Jessica's wet cloak began to steam as the temperature rose.

"Nearly there now," said Miss Strega.

Moments later, half a dozen little islands came into view. They dazzled like green and white fruit drops scattered over a turquoise mat. Jessica and Miss Strega tweaked their *Pause* twigs and hung in the sky admiring the long white sandy beaches fringed with palms

and dotted with all sorts of witchy people flying kites, building sandcastles and paddling in the shallows. Water-skiers skimmed between the islands leaving silver streaks in their wake.

"Wow!" said Jessica.

"Hu-eeeeet!" whistled Berkeley.

"Merrowwww!" purred Felicity.

"Well, tickle me pink with a flying fish!" exclaimed Miss Strega. "It's charming!"

"And look at that!" Jessica pointed to the largest of the islands, Charm Major. On top of the highest cliff there was a tall slender whitewashed lighthouse. A weather vane in the shape of a witch on her broomstick (right way up, of course) swung gently in the sea breeze. And there, on the look-out platform, was an extraordinary creature waving a Witches World Wide flag and shouting through a megaphone, "PERMISSION FOR LANDING GRANTED."

Jessica grinned at Miss Strega. "Is that Pelagia?"

"The very same, and she likes nothing better than a stylish landing so let's dip and bob prettily as we approach."

Pelagia was quite unlike any witch that Jessica had ever seen. She wore knee-length shorts,

a black bandanna and a cloak patterned with sea horses and starfish. Her legs were bare and her toenails painted blue. She had orange freckles, mad hair, gold hoop earrings and lots of charm bracelets that tinkled when she moved.

"Welcome to the Charm Archipelago, me dears," she said as she hugged Miss Strega, patted Felicity and Berkeley and shook Jessica's hand. "We'll get cracking right away."

Pelagia set off at a blistering pace, whizzing down the banisters of the spiral staircase with Jessica and Miss Strega sliding behind her as fast as they could.

"That will be your room..." said Pelagia, pointing through an open door where Jessica could see a pair of hammocks strung up between two round porthole windows, "...and that is my Control Room."

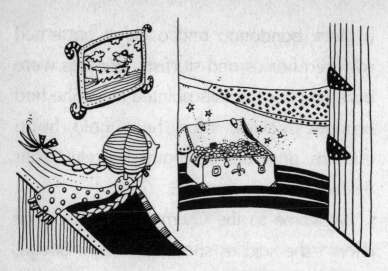

Jessica got a glimpse of another hammock hanging above a large mahogany sea-chest with gilded brass corners. The lid was raised and it seemed to be full of rolled up maps, gold coins, pearls and other jewels. Her eyes nearly popped out of her head.

"Hey," she whispered over her shoulder to Miss Strega., "look at all that treasure." But, even as she spoke, the chest gave a little giggle and slowly closed all by itself.

When they reached the ground floor and jumped off the handrail, there was another surprise. A large arched door swung open on a very busy, very noisy kitchen. A floor brush and dustpan were sweeping up a pile of sand that had blown in under the door. A parade of plates and cups were sailing across the room from the draining board to the dresser. A tray was busily piling itself up with tumblers, jugs of cool drinks, an ice bucket and some curly straws.

"Good show," Pelagia beamed. "Come out to the garden as soon as you can."

Jessica tugged at Miss Strega's elbow. "Who is she speaking to? Does she have an invisible helper?"

Miss Strega tapped the side of her long nose and laid a long finger on her lips, as if she knew perfectly well what was going on.

"Pelagia," Jessica began, "how do the dustpan and brush and the cups and the tray...?"

Pelagia chuckled. "Charming, aren't they, like every well-run home." And, without another word of explanation, she hurried Jessica and Miss Strega out into the lighthouse garden.

"Do make yourself comfortable, Miss Strega," she said, pointing at a deckchair under a huge umbrella with a thatch of palm leaves. She clapped her hands and the tray with a jug of iced fruit cocktails and a large platter piled high with mango, coconut and pineapple floated towards them.

"This is going to be wicked," Jessica thought, wondering if she should start with a slice of mango or a wedge of pineapple, but Pelagia gently caught her by the elbow.

"Our classes start at once," she said as she steered her towards the garden gate. "You won't need your broom, me dear, and you'll probably be more comfortable without your shoes too."

Chapter Three

Jessica followed Pelagia down to the edge of the cliff and clambered after her as she swung on to an iron ladder that led down to the beach below.

"This is where I landed many moons ago,"

Pelagia explained as she held out her hand for Jessica to jump off the bottom rung. "It's a marvellous beach for lucky pebbles." She knelt down and began to pick up smooth stones which she set out in groups of three and then in complicated interlocking circles.

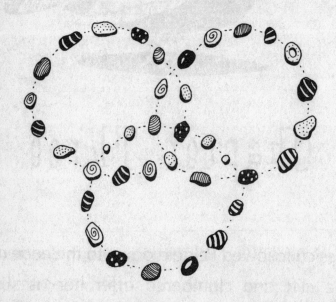

"Miss Strega said you used to be a pirate," Jessica remarked casually as she knelt down to watch.

Pelagia's bracelets rattled. "Never say pirate, me dear, say sallee-rover. But yes, Miss Strega is right. I spent years on the high seas, seeing the sights from old Cathay to Valparaiso."

"And why did you give it up?"

"We'll leave that story for another day," said Pelagia with a pained expression. Then she closed her eyes and began to chant:

"Circles within circles
Of pebbles in trebles
Banish all harm and
Conjure a Charm."

Within moments, Pelagia seemed to have fallen asleep. Jessica looked about her. She listened to the froo-froh of the wind in the palm trees and the rumbling, gurgling noises coming from her tummy.

"I'm really hungry," Jessica murmured, remembering the slices of mango and pineapple. "I wonder when we have supper."

Berkeley peeked her head out of Jessica's pocket. "Hu-eet, hu-eeet?" she whistled, offering Jessica a pinch of bird seed.

Immediately, a terrible hullabaloo started up in a nearby tree. "Clear off," something squawked. "Buzz off. Sling your hook."

"Umm, Pelagia?" Jessica said, stroking Berkeley's neck feathers to calm her down. "Someone in that tree is being very rude to us." Pelagia opened her eyes. "That's Josephine being silly about Berkeley. She's not used to bird visitors."

"Is Josephine another witch?"

"Not at all. She's my mascot, a hornbill. She's in a hollow inside that tree where she's laid her egg and she'll stay sealed up in it until her chick is ready to fly."

"Sealed inside the tree? She must be starving."

Pelagia laughed. "Not at all. You can help me feed her later on. Do you see that hard red and yellow thing poking out of the slit in the trunk – that's her bill. But now, back to work."

She waved a hand over the three circles of stones. "Three is a perfect number, don't you agree? It has a beginning, a middle and an end. And so many good things come in threes."

"Like the two sides and the middle of a cheese sandwich?" Jessica suggested. Her tummy grumbled even louder. "A knife and a fork and a spoon? Toast and butter and marmalade? Sausage, egg and chips?"

Pelagia's bracelets rattled.

"Oops. Sorry." Jessica turned a little pink.

Pelagia smiled. "It's a good idea to carry a lucky stone before eating in a strange place. That's an elementary rule for travelling witches. We'll brew up once you've chosen your stone. Any one of these will protect you from harm but, if you select the right one, you'll be able to use it as a conjuring stone as well."

Jessica examined the pebbles. At first they all seemed to be the same, sort of brown and speckled. But as she picked them up and looked harder, she could see they were all different. Some had little flecks of white, or red, or black. Some were nearly completely brown. Some stones had shiny bits that glinted in the sunlight. One of them had a very tiny little hole. Jessica stroked her cheek with it and blew through the hole. "This is it," she said firmly. "This is definitely it."

"In that case—" said Pelagia, springing to her feet.

"Oh, good, thought Jessica, food at last!"

"—I'll give you your Timetable and the Task List."

"Timetable? Task list?" Jessica sighed. Charm School sounded as if it was going to be very hard work.

Pelagia rummaged in the pockets of her starfish cloak and drew out several rolls of crisp brown paper that looked as if they had been soaked in tea.

"This is a navigation map of the Archipelago," she explained as she handed Jessica three sheets. "This is your Timetable and finally, this is the Task List. By the way, will you want pins or pendants when you've finished?"

Jessica wrinkled her nose.

Pelagia rattled her charm bracelets. "You know, pendants like these to wear on your wrists. Or perhaps you'd prefer pins to wear on your cape?"

"Pins," said Jessica, beaming. "Definitely pins."

"Right! That's decided. Now lets make that brew."

Charm School already sounded more promising.

Chapter Four

After supper, Jessica was very keen to study her Timetable and Task List. She was also very keen to try out her hammock so she went off to her room. After her umpteenth attempt to climb into it, she felt like a winded starfish trying to climb into a moving onion bag. Again and again, she grasped the side rope with two hands, hauled herself off the ground, tried to get one knee inside and then the other, but every time she would overshoot

and tumble down the other side. This of course made the hammock sway and rock violently. Then she tried something different. She ran backwards and threw herself into the hammock with a sort of high jump scissors technique. The world started spinning, but after a few minutes the hammock settled into a gentle relaxing swing. She had made it!

"Tut-tut," said Miss Strega, suddenly appearing at her side. "You do make things difficult for yourself." With that, she picked up her broomstick, flew up above her hammock, paused, descended, settled herself comfortably and ordered the broomstick to wait beneath the window for further instructions.

Jessica sighed loudly. Sometimes she completely forgot she was a GASP of BR(EATH), that is to say, a Graduate Airborne Spinner and Pilot of the Broom Riders: (Earth And The Heavens).

"Now, Jess," said Miss Strega, lying back on her cushions. "Tell us what Pelagia has in store for you."

Jessica began to read aloud.

The Lighthou
The Char

DAILY TIMETABLE FOR MISS JES

From now

When?	What happens?
09:00-10:00.	charming with inca
10:05-11:05	charms and Talisme
11:05-11:30	BREAK
11:30-12:30	Easy Ways to cha
12:35-13:30	Oracles and Fortu
13:30-14:30	LUNCH

Afternoons will be spent on p
Pins or pendants will be awarded for successfu

The Four Ch

1. charmers-in-Training must not use b
2. Mascots must be kept strictly unde
3. The Lighthouse Control Room is OUT
4.

Charm School
rchipelago

DIAMOND WITCH-IN-TRAINING

whenever

	Where?
ons	The Music Room
	The Art Room
ur Home	The Kitchen
lling	To be decided

al exercises and/or excursions.
pletion of the witch-in-training's personal tasks.

School Rules

sticks, wands or Spell Books.
trol.
BOUNDS

"The fourth rule is missing," Jessica told Miss Strega. " I wonder what it is?"

"Never mind, it can't be that important. Anyway, it all sounds pretty impressive."

Jessica didn't answer. "Too many hard words," she was thinking. "Oracles, Incantations, Talismans. Aaarrggh."

When Jessica arrived in the Music Room the following morning, she found Pelagia sitting in the middle of the floor, painting her toenails Electric Red.

"Good morning, me dear. We'll start our first Incantation as soon as the band is here and my nails have dried. Please leave the door open."

A few moments later, Jessica was rather startled when a procession of instruments began to drift in, in twos and threes, like an orchestra arriving for a morning rehearsal, and set about tuning themselves.

There were lutes and flutes, zithers and round-bellied mandolins, fiddles and fiddlesticks, tubas, cymbals, castanets, a huge kettledrum, two conch horns, a glockenspiel, a bazooka and a didgeridoo.

"A Charm or Incantation," Pelagia began, shouting over the crashing cymbals and the throbbing of the didgeridoo, "is a combination..." The rest of her words were drowned out by the kettledrum.

"What?" yelled Jessica, cupping one ear with her hand.

Pelagia's bracelets rattled. "Can I PLEASE have a bit of shush?" she demanded. She struck her music stand with her conductor's baton (which was, Jessica noticed, exactly like a magic wand). All the instruments fell silent.

"As I was saying, a Charm or Incantation is a combination of words to make magic. The best ones are always set to music. Do you play a musical instrument?"

"The recorder," said Jessica, wincing, "but not very well."

"Just stick to the singing then," said Pelagia. "Now, today, as every day, our first task is to make up an Incantation to keep everyone safe at sea. Is there much traffic out there?"

Jessica looked out of the window. "Lots and lots. There are a few wind surfers and WHOA, one of them is heading directly for a barge full of coconuts. Then, there are two goblins riding a green inflatable crocodile and a boat that's pulling some young witches along on a floating banana. OH MY! WHOOPS! That was a near miss! Those goblins DELIBERATELY

tried to capsize the banana. Then there's a pair of water-skiers. OH DEAR! One of them has just come off her skis. And a two-witch canoe race has just started from Lesser Charm pier but, OH GOLLY! Miss Strega is lolling about on a Lilo and drifting right into the middle of them. And WOW! Is that a shark fin, near where the wizard is laying lobster pots."

"Lots of trouble brewing by the sound of it. There's no time to lose." Pelagia tapped her music stand with her baton. "Line up, everyone. Jessica, you lead. You'll find the words just form themselves. On the count of three. One, two, three."

At once, the orchestra began drumming and strumming, jamming and slamming, banging and clanging, tooting and fluting. Berkeley, usually a solo singer, joined in enthusiastically too as Jessica intoned:

"Wey-hey-hey,
Roll and go-oh-oh,
Clip along smartly, not too slow-oh-oh.
Gentle waves will rock you,
No mean wind will knock you,
As long as ALL of you,
Give way to Charm."

"And fol de rol, and a bottle of rum," Pelagia added with a flourish of her baton while the kettledrum brought everything to an end with a fantastic drum roll.

Jessica and Pelagia rushed to the window. Beneath them, everyone happily fished, sailed, floated, skied, swam, canoed or just lolled in perfect harmony.

"Charming!" Pelagia declared. "Take a bow, Jessica. That will surely keep them all from colliding with one another for the time being. Now, I must reset the Charms for the cleaning and cooking equipment in the kitchen. It's very time-consuming but I have to do it every day, just like the Safety-at-Sea Incantation. I'll see you in the Art Room in five minutes and we'll make a start on Talismans."

Chapter Five

The days flew past. Jessica invented a new Incantation every morning. She made an abracadabra charm to hang around her neck to protect her from toothache:

Abracadabra
Abracadabr
Abracadab
Abracada
Abracad
Abraca
Abrac
Abra
Abr
Ab
A

She learned to keep a nutmeg in her pocket to prevent hair tangles – a Charm you might find very useful if you have long plaits like Jessica. (Fortunately Berkeley rather liked the smell so didn't mind that her pocket was getting a bit crowded what with the nutmeg, the lucky pebble, the pocket fluff bedding and the store of bird seed.)

She began to tell fortunes: reading the lines on Miss Strega and Pelagia's palms and also looking closely at hornbill droppings! The Easy Ways to Charm Your Home class was brilliant. Jessica learnt to order cold drinks and snacks to fly to her with a snap of her fingers. She could also charm her hammock to lower and raise itself when she wanted to get in or out of bed.

Oracles were tricky though. They were special places where people could go to ask important questions like, *"Should I get my hair cut?"* But the answer was always in riddles. For example, when Jessica asked the Mynah Bird Oracle, *"Will Berkeley be upset if I get a second mascot?"* it had replied: "Three into two won't go. Put down your nought.

Three into twenty goes six times and two over. Bring down your nought. Three into twenty goes six times and two over. Bring down your nought..." It went on and on like that for hours, until everybody was going crazy and screaming PLEASE BE QUIET. In the end, Miss Strega put a Silent Spell on it.

But the best thing of all about Charm School was making Talismans. It was like making models in plasticine or papier maché, only more useful. If you made a spider Talisman, for instance, and put it in your bathroom, then no spiders with skinny legs could sit in your wash basin or crawl out of the plughole of your bath.

One busy morning, Jessica made three spider Talismans; one each for her mum, Pelagia and Miss Strega who *all* hated spiders. Then she went in search of lunch.

Jessica found Pelagia and Miss Strega in the kitchen, supervising a picnic hamper filling itself up with roast chicken and hard-boiled eggs, tuna sandwiches, home-made coconut biscuits, peaches and bottles of lemonade. Felicity was sitting on top of the fridge, her tail flicking furiously at the feast floating by. Berkeley was pecking crumbs off the floor.

"This afternoon," Pelagia announced with a loud rattle of charm bracelets, "we are going on a witch hunt on Charm Minor." She pointed out of the window at the tiniest island in the Archipelago.

"Fantastic," Jessica cheered. "I'll fetch my broomstick."

"No need, me dear. No one ever travels by broomstick around here. We'll take the Tub."

The Tub turned out to be Pelagia's boat. Of course it was not like any old rowing boat. In the first place, it was round and flat-bottomed, a bit like something that Jessica's mother might plant flowers in.

Miss Strega looked at it with horror. She rubbed her chin and tapped her nose. "I'm a broomstick kind of person, me," she said but Jessica immediately hopped in and reached for the oars.

"Can I row? It looks easy peasy."

Pelagia jangled her bracelets but said nothing.

In fact, rowing was not easy peasy. Jessica soon found herself going round and round in circles. And the more she tried to stop making circles, the more circles she made. It was terribly embarrassing. She even thought about activating her Super-Duper De-Luxe Guaranteed-Invisibility-When-You-Need-It Cape.

Then she had an idea. "Perhaps the Tub is spooked. Perhaps Pelagia has put a Talisman or a Charm on it."

She set down the oars, held her lucky

pebble Charm tightly in one hand and carefully chose her words:

"Talisman, talisman, come to my aid,
Undo the charm Pelagia's made."

Instantly, the oars began to slice cleanly through the sea, splish, splash, bowling along at a cracking pace towards Charm Minor.

"Well spotted, Jessica," said Pelagia approvingly, reaching under her seat and picking up a little wax model of someone rowing the Tub. "Ever since a shipwrecked goblin turned up here once and tried to steal the Tub, I've kept this Talisman on board so that no one but me can use it. If they do, they just go round and round in circles all day. So, you've earned your first pin."

"Oh goody," said Jessica but she couldn't help wondering if the goblin was the same one that she had once ejected into the sea.

As they pulled into the harbour on Charm Minor, Pelagia jumped on to the pier and secured the boat's mooring rope. Miss Strega, Jessica, Felicity and Berkeley clambered unsteadily on to dry land, all of them looking a bit green.

"There's a lot to be said for flying," Miss Strega muttered. "You should try it. I can send you a besom if you like. £4.99 or £8.00 for two."

Pelagia just smiled. "Now, Jessica, let's start the witch hunt before we have our picnic. We'll give you ten minutes and then we're coming to find you."

"You're hunting me?" said Jessica.

"Of course, you're *it*, aren't you? Now,

off you go, chop, chop, me dear. And remember," she shouted as Jessica ran off, "Charming is the name of the game."

Jessica ran along the long flat sandy beach. "Nowhere to hide here," she thought.

She gazed up at the tall trunks of the coconut palms. "Impossible to climb," she decided.

She scrunched up her eyes and searched in vain for a building. "There is absolutely nothing to hide *in* and nothing to hide *behind*."

Far off, she could hear Pelagia and Miss Strega shouting: "Coming to get you, ready or not."

In desperation, she peered into a cleft in the rock face on the beach. "You couldn't really call this a cave, it's just a big crack," she said aloud to Berkeley. "If you ask me, Charm Minor is a silly place to have a witch hunt."

Suddenly, a hornbill poked her huge red and yellow beak out of a tree hollow and squawked bad-temperedly. "You've woken me up. Do you know how long it takes for me to get to sleep in this hot cramped scratchy nest?"

"I'm very sorry," Jessica said politely. "Are you from this island?"

"I've been hanging around here all summer, all summer," the hornbill screeched.

"Then, perhaps you could suggest somewhere for me to hide? You see,

my personal trainers
are on a witch hunt
and I don't know
where to go."

"Charming is the name of
the game," shrieked the hornbill. "Charming is
the name of the game."

Jessica twisted the end of her plait
around her finger and pondered. Then she
tapped her nose in a Miss Strega-like kind
of way and drew her lucky stone Charm
from her pocket again.

"Perhaps I can conjure up a hiding-place,"
she thought. "Would you mind if I used
a corner of your nest-opening for a
while, Ms Hornbill?"

Hours later, Miss Strega abruptly
sat down in the shade of a palm
tree and threw off her shoes.

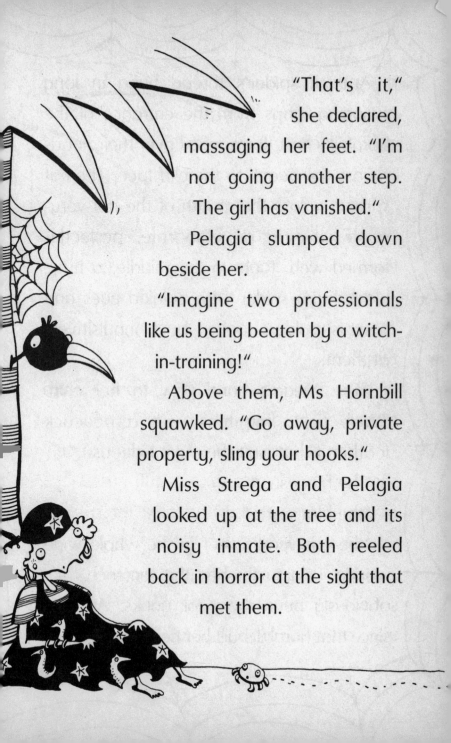

"That's it," she declared, massaging her feet. "I'm not going another step. The girl has vanished."

Pelagia slumped down beside her.

"Imagine two professionals like us being beaten by a witch-in-training!"

Above them, Ms Hornbill squawked. "Go away, private property, sling your hooks."

Miss Strega and Pelagia looked up at the tree and its noisy inmate. Both reeled back in horror at the sight that met them.

A thick spider's thread hung in long swinging loops from the entrance of the hornbill's nest. It trapezed over their heads across the beach to the cliff face. There it spread across the mouth of the not-very-good cave in an elaborate, perfectly-formed web. Right in the middle, a huge black hairy spider with bulging eyes and hefty shoulders looked back inquisitively at them.

Miss Strega's hand flew to her chin. "Well, tickle my toes with a peacock feather if that isn't the most hideous..."

"the biggest..."

"the blackest..."

"the cheekiest spider in the whole wide world." Pelagia finished the sentence. "It's obviously been there for yonks. At least since that hornbill built her nest weeks ago."

From behind the spider's web, there came an odd little explosion.

"Did you hear that?" asked Miss Strega. "A sort of sneezy giggle?"

"A bit of a choke mixed with a titter?" replied Pelagia.

They clambered to their feet and began to tiptoe away from the beach.

"Da-da-da! Gotcha!" shouted Jessica, jumping out from the not-very-good cave behind the web. "It wasn't a real spider. And not a real web. They're magic. I just conjured them up so you wouldn't see me in this tootsy cave. Only Ms Hornbill and her nest are real."

"Shiver me timbers," declared Pelagia, blinking. "The bird-in-the-nest, the nest-in-the-tree, the web-from-the-branch, the spider-at-the-cave-door Charm. I am most impressed. We'll have to give you another pin for that. That makes the final score today: Witch-in-training – two; Witch trainers – zero."

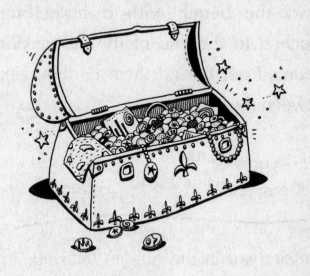

Chapter Six

One afternoon, Jessica found herself alone.
Berkeley had made friends with a flute and
was in the Music Room. Pelagia had gone to
visit Josephine who had just hatched her egg.
Felicity and Miss Strega had decided to do

some advertising and were flying up and down the beach with a huge banner attached to the end of the broomstick. It streamed out behind them as they zipped between the islands.

Miss Strega's Hardware Shop (estd. 991)
The best for all your witchy needs.

Jessica sat in the garden thinking. And what she was thinking about was Rule Number Three:

The Lighthouse Control Room is strictly OUT OF BOUNDS.

Ever since she had spotted that treasure chest beneath Pelagia's hammock, she had been itching to look inside it.

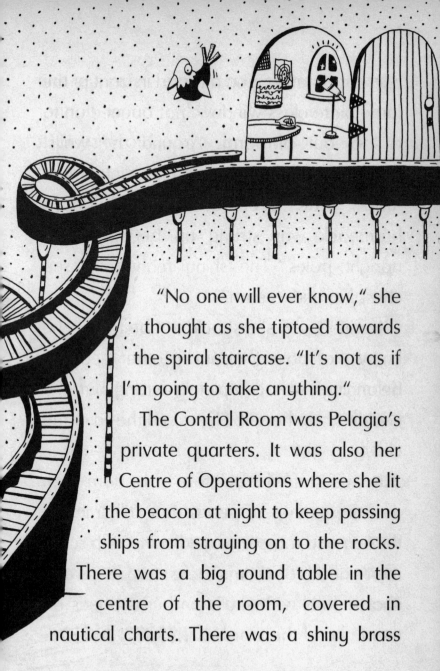

"No one will ever know," she thought as she tiptoed towards the spiral staircase. "It's not as if I'm going to take anything."

The Control Room was Pelagia's private quarters. It was also her Centre of Operations where she lit the beacon at night to keep passing ships from straying on to the rocks. There was a big round table in the centre of the room, covered in nautical charts. There was a shiny brass telescope standing on a tripod in front of the large plate glass window that opened on to a look-out platform. Around the walls, banks of monitors winked and blinked and made little beeping noises. Pelagia's hammock was strung up between two upright poles. The shiny mahogany sea chest lay underneath.

Jessica knew she should not be there. She knew that poking about in other people's belongings was completely wrong but she couldn't help herself. She raised the lid of the chest.

It was stuffed from top to bottom with treasure, strings of pearls that still smelt of the sea and masses of gold coins with scary men's heads on them. There were maps and charts, too, with skulls and crossbones on them… and the words X MARKS THE SPOT.

Underneath everything, there was a bright blue cloth bag tied at the neck with a silver string. It squirmed and sighed when Jessica picked it up as if it held something alive...

...and as soon as she began to undo the string, strange noises began to well up from the bottom of the bag. In no time at all, the Control Room was filled with the most tremendous roaring and shrieking and huffing and puffing. Pelagia's hammock began to swing wildly. Maps and charts blew off the table. The doors on to the terrace banged open. One by one, out of the bag, came all the cross, bad-tempered winds that had ever blown around the earth, all of them howling and yelling and screaming as they escaped. Jessica, with her cape flapping around her face, tried to stuff the bag back into the chest but it had got tangled around one of her wrists. Suddenly she was picked up like a leaf in an autumn storm and carried off through the open doors – and she didn't even have her broomstick!

"Help!" she roared as a gale blew her clean off the lighthouse. "Help!" she roared again as a hurricane tossed her from one end of the Archipelago to the other, and back again.

With her free hand, Jessica felt in her pocket for Berkeley. "Aren't you supposed to protect me in storms?" she protested. But of course Berkeley wasn't there. He was in the Music Room trilling away with the magic flute.

Luckily, all the sea traffic was still under the spell of the morning incantation so it carried on sailing and surfing and skiing and fishing, completely unaware of the hullabaloo above its head.

Only Miss Strega realized what was going on and Fast-Forwarded towards Jessica. Jessica saw her coming. She saw that Miss Strega was bearing down on her like a witch on the warpath. The last time she had seen Miss Strega look so angry was the day she had turned Jessica into a pumpkin. (Of course Jessica had turned Miss Strega into a wasp, first, so she had every right to be cross.)

"Please don't transform me into something nasty," she thought as the North wind hurled freezing rain at her and flung her into a spin above Charm Minor. Grabbing the ends of her Super-Duper De-Luxe Guaranteed-Invisibility-When-You-Need-It cape, she pleaded, "I need invisibility. I need it right now."

Immediately, a hot little monsoon breeze caught her and dumped her into the top leaves of a swaying coconut palm. Miss Strega screeched to a halt beside it.

"Jessica, I know you're there. Reappear at once. I don't want to have to say it again. Moonrays and marrowbones, Jessica! You will be *very* sorry if you don't reappear."

Jessica reappeared.

"Let go of the bag," Miss Strega ordered. "Jessica, let go of the bag. Drop the bag, Jessica. Yes, on the sand."

Jessica undid the string from her wrist and flung the bag as far away as she could. At Miss Strega's command, all the winds scuttled back into it. Then she flew her broomstick around the palm tree and hauled Jessica on to it.

"Not a word! Not a single word!" she warned her before zooming back to the lighthouse.

There was a Special Meeting after supper. Jessica apologized four hundred and forty four times until Pelagia said that was enough.

"You had no choice. It's a very spiteful bag with a mean Spell on it. Do you remember you once asked me why I gave up being a sallee-rover?"

"Yes," said Jessica, "but you didn't say."

"It was like this. Mean Jack, the skipper on my last ship, never paid his crew their fair wages. One night, I crept into his cabin and took the swag bag that he kept under his bunk."

"Treasure?" asked Jessica.

"No treasure at all, me dear, just trouble, for it was that very bag with every nasty breeze, gale, squall, typhoon and hurricane that ever blew inside it. Mean Jack had tricked them into the bag so that he could get his treasure home safely without being delayed by storms. Unfortunately, just as you found out, the minute I undid the silver string, out they all flew, making such a hugger-mugger that the ocean boiled up and I was blown clean off the ship. For three days and three nights, I was hurled from one wild ocean to another until finally I managed to charm the winds back into the bag. That was when I was washed up here."

"And that's when you decided to give up being a pirate, I mean, a sallee-rover."

"Yes indeedy," Pelagia agreed. "From that day to this, I have been Charming."

"I think I will be Charming from now on too," murmured Jessica, shamefaced.

"I should say so," said Miss Strega, nodding vigorously. "Otherwise we shall have to make little Jessica Talismans to keep you out of places you don't belong!"

Chapter Seven

"You may find this useful when you're out and about in the Tub this afternoon," said Pelagia, coming into the kitchen and placing a brown bottle on the draining board. "Just one or two tablespoonfuls and

I guarantee you won't be seasick."

Jessica, who was blowing dozens of soap bubbles as part of a project she was doing for her Easy Ways to Charm Your Home class, put down her bubble wand. She picked up the bottle, read the label – Distilled Salmagundi, the Sailor's Friend – uncorked it and sniffed. "It smells really nasty," she said, her eyes watering. "What on earth is in it?"

"Essence of flying fish, cabbage, turtle meat, mangoes, extra hot mustard, pigeons, pigs' trotters, hard ship's biscuit, gur cake, olive oil, and a most secret ingredient that I cannot tell you about."

"How many spoonfuls do I take?"

"*You* don't have to take it at all. You just pour it overboard at the start of your journey. It gives the sea such indigestion it has to lie down for a nap. It'll be flat as a pancake all the time you are at sea."

Jessica and Miss Strega exchanged a look. The look meant, is Pelagia serious?

"Moonrays and marrowbones, Pelagia," Miss Strega exclaimed. "Why would Jessica be running about in the Tub on her own, anyway?"

Pelagia pushed all her bracelets up to her elbow and pulled the plug on Jessica's soapy water. "Haven't you told Miss Strega about your last task, Jessica?"

Jessica wriggled her nose. "I'm going to visit an Oracle."

"But you can't stand Oracles." Miss Strega reminded her. "Remember what happened with the Mynah Bird Oracle? And why do you need the Tub?"

"Because the Oracle is on Outer Charm,"

Jessica explained. "Do you remember that there were four rules?"

Miss Strega nodded. "But the fourth rule was missing."

"Well, the problem is that someone borrowed it and didn't give it back and Pelagia can't remember it any more. So my last task is to find the Oracle on Outer Charm and ask it what the rule was. If I can work out the riddle, I get double pins."

"You're going on your own? In the Tub? Without a broomstick or a wand?" Miss Strega peered at Jessica over her glasses.

Jessica nodded three times.

"Then you had better take that salmagundi," said Miss Strega, "and your lucky pebble *and* your hat. The sun on outer Charm is very strong. I'm going for a little zizz." And off she went without even wishing Jessica *Good Luck*.

Once Jessica had undone the Charm on the oars of the Tub and poured the salmagundi on the waves, she set off for Outer Charm. It would have been quite pleasant tootling about the islands if there hadn't been so many butterflies in her tummy. An albatross wheeled around in the sky above her and shoals of silvery flying fish leapt in and out

of the water. A dolphin, which had a Miss Strega look about it, even kept her company all the way to the harbour on Outer Charm.

Outer Charm had a fantastic beach with a huge rock pool. Little miniature lantern fish with glowing tails darted around in it. There were starfish, sea horses and scuttling crabs.

Jessica was so engrossed she had almost forgotten the reason for her journey. Then a strange creature with bristling tentacles crawled out of the depths of the pool and clambered up on to a seaweedy rock beside her.

Jessica stared suspiciously at it. "Are you some sort of a water hedgehog?"

"I am the Giant Sea Anemone, the voice of the Oracle," the creature replied, looking rather offended with its tentacles all a-quiver. "Why are you here?"

"I am Jessica Diamond, Witch-in-Training," Jessica replied, "and I've come to ask you a question. *What was Rule Number Four?*"

The Giant Sea Anemone pursed its watery lips. "When the bats flit by the beacon and the patient gecko shows her tongue, then shall all but saved charms fade."

Jessica knitted her brows. "Is that it? Have you finished?"

But the Giant Sea Anemone said nothing more and, after a few seconds, slid noiselessly back into the pool.

Jessica thoughtfully chewed on the end of a plait.

*

"So," Jessica later explained to Pelagia, "I think this is what the Oracle means. *'When the bats flit by the beacon.'* OK, the beacon means the lighthouse light and that's only lit at night-time when it's dark. That's also when the bats come out. *'And the patient gecko shows her tongue'.* You know how the geckos wait patiently beneath the light to catch passing flies by flicking out their long tongues? So the Oracle means during the night. *'Then shall all but saved charms fade'.* Well, that means that Charms won't last unless you save them. It's just like saving your work on a computer. So the fourth rule must have been: Save all your Charms or they will be lost overnight."

"So that's why I have to keep resetting the housework Charms every day and the

Safety-at-Sea incantations! Silly me." Pelagia poured some tropical fruit punch into three tall glasses and passed them round. "That certainly deserves a drink and... double pins."

"And you'll never guess what," Jessica added. "A dolphin followed me all the way to Outer Charm and back. It was looking after me, I think."

"A dolphin? Fancy that!" Miss Strega remarked, picking a stray piece of seaweed out of her hair.

Pelagia's bracelets tinkled. "You wouldn't know anything about that, me dear, would you?" she asked.

"Me, why should I?" protested Miss Strega, stepping out of a puddle of sea water that was spreading round her feet.

Chapter Eight

It had been another perfect day in the Charm Archipelago. Jessica was sitting on a deck chair, watching the sun set and dribbling warm sand over her toes. Berkeley was singing from the top of the flag pole on the lighthouse and Felicity was playing pounce with the coconuts that dropped on to the sand. Miss Strega was cackling quietly as she read her book, *Spelling Confidential – the true story behind the scenes at Coven Garden*, while Pelagia was painting her toenails Pearly Plum. A flock of knock-kneed pink flamingos had swooped in to fish in the shallows. A perfect day.

"I want to go home," said Jessica in a small voice.

"What's that, Jess?" said Miss Strega, looking up from her book.

"What did you say?" asked Pelagia, replacing the brush in the bottle of varnish.

"I want to be home, in my room, with my own things," Jessica repeated. "It's very lovely here and I have enjoyed myself but I miss my home and the park and working out the meaning of the labels in the hardware shop. I miss the cats. I miss flying my broomstick. I even miss the rain."

"So," said Miss Strega and Pelagia together, "that means it's whenever."

"Whenever?"

"That's what I put on the notice, don't you remember? That we'd be *back whenever.*"

"And *I* put it on your timetable – *from now until whenever.*"

Miss Strega closed her book and stood up. "We'd better go and pack. Come along, Felicity, leave that coconut alone."

Jessica and Miss Strega mounted their broomsticks and hovered side by side on the

top viewing platform of the lighthouse, ready for take-off.

"There's just one thing we have to do before you leave," Pelagia said. "Your pins, me dear," and she handed Jessica a little goody bag tied at the neck with a purple and green ribbon. "You've won the coloured Hornbill that squawks to warn you of trouble ahead and the Lantern Fish that glows in the dark so you can read in bed or on a flight. And the Incredible Golden Date that you can nibble if you are hungry without it ever getting smaller."

"Thank you!" said Jessica. "They're brilliant."

"And there's lots more you can work out for yourself when you get home. But just before you go—" Pelagia delved into the pocket of her star-fish cloak and pulled out a little white lighthouse pin that was exactly like *her* lighthouse "—this is just a little going-away present from me."

"I love it," gasped Jessica, "but what does it do?"

"It's a Safe Harbour Charm. When you wear it, it will always get you safely home," Pelagia replied as she pinned the lighthouse on Jessica's cape.

Then she wiped a tear from her eye,

patted Felicity and Berkeley, kissed Miss Strega and gave Jessica a big hug. "Now, me dear, just blink, count to ten and off you go. Safe home."

Jessica blinked and silently counted to ten.

When she opened her eyes, she and Miss Strega were flying low over Jessica's front garden. All the cats in the neighbourhood – big fluffy marmalades, sleek Siamese, silver tabbies and black moggies – were standing on the garage roof to greet her. Her mother's car was in the drive. She could

smell baking. Someone had stuck a "Welcome Home Jessica" poster on her bedroom window. It was raining.

"Wow!" she exclaimed.

"Hu-eet, hu-eet," agreed Berkeley, poking her head out of Jessica's pocket.

"Well bowl me over with an apple pip!" exclaimed Miss Strega before she zoomed off to the High Street. "That pin's just got us halfway round the globe in ten seconds. Is that Charming or what? I need a good stiff brew to get my breath back."

Grinning from ear to ear, Jessica waved goodbye. Then she swooped down to the drive, hopped off her broom and dashed inside out of the wet.